Enid Blyton's
NODDY
and his Car

Illustrated by Edgar Hodges

Macdonald Purnell

0 361 07177 9
Text copyright © 1986 Darrell Waters Limited
Illustrations copyright © 1986 Macdonald and Co
(Publishers) Limited
This edition first published 1986 by Purnell Books
a division of Macdonald and Co (Publishers) Limited
Greater London House
Hampstead Road
London NW1 7QX
a BPCC plc company
Made and printed in Great Britain

British Library Cataloguing in Publication Data
Blyton, Enid
  Noddy and his car.–(Noddy library; 3)
  I. Title   II. Series
  823'.912[J] PZ7

One morning Noddy woke up feeling very happy. He sat up in bed and wondered why.

"Why do I feel so glad?" he giggled. "Why do I want to sing and shout all of a sudden?"

Then he suddenly remembered. To make sure he wasn't dreaming, he put his head out of the window and looked down into the garden. It was true, his own little red and yellow car was still standing there. Noddy gazed at it in delight.

"I've got a car of my very own. Today I will be a taxi-driver and give everyone in Toyland a ride!"

His round wooden head began to nod madly. It always did when he was feeling very pleased about something. He couldn't help it, he was just made that way. His neck was joined to his body by a little spring.

Noddy whistled happily to himself as he put on his bright red shoes and tied up the blue laces.

"My car is all red and yellow and bright and shining! I shall keep it very clean. What a good thing it didn't rain in the night," he thought as he pulled his hat on. "My car would have got very wet. I'd better build a garage for it," he giggled as he ran about making his breakfast. The bell at the top of his hat jingled merrily, while Noddy hummed a happy tune.

Soon Noddy heard the milkman calling "Milko!" and he ran to the door to collect the milk.

"One bottle please…and how do you like my car?" he spluttered.

"It's wonderful!" laughed the milkman. "Is it the one the toys gave you for helping them to find the cars that the goblins stole from Bobby Bear's garage?"

"Yes it is!" said Noddy, nodding happily. "It was so kind of them to give me a car, Mr Milko. I'm going to be a taxi-driver and give them all rides in it. I'll polish it every day, and when I've earned some money I'll buy some bricks and build a little garage to put it in at night."

"I'll tell everybody you're a taxi-driver then," said the milkman kindly. "How much are you going to charge for each journey, little Noddy?"

"I haven't thought yet," said Noddy, taking his bottle of milk. "Have you got any ideas?"

"What about a fare of one penny for the journey all the way there and one penny for the journey all the way back?" said the milkman rubbing his chin thoughtfully.

"That's what I'll charge then!" smiled Noddy, and he thanked

the milkman for his help. "I'll just get the money for the milk."

"Oh, I don't want any this morning," laughed Mr Milko. "Just let me tap your head, and set it nodding!" Noddy was pleased to oblige. Mr Milko gave his head a tap and it nodded so much that the bell on his hat tinkled like a musical box.

"Thank you Noddy. You've made my day!" laughed the milkman again.

"Oh that's all right, Mr Milko! Don't forget to tell everyone I'm a taxi-driver now and I'm waiting for passengers!"

"Leave it to me," smiled the milkman, then he walked down the path shouting "Milko! Milko!" at the top of his voice. Noddy watched him as he delivered his milk down the street.

"I hope my first passenger comes soon!" he whispered.

Noddy tidied his house then polished his beautiful car, singing a happy song. Mr Tubby, the teddy bear who lived next door, put his head out of the window and waved.

"That's a nice song! I've never heard of a singing taxi-driver before. Have you had any passengers yet?"

"Not yet," said Noddy, "but I'm waiting. I'm sure someone will come soon. I'll drive my car out of the garden and on to the road, then it will be ready."

And sure enough, as soon as he'd driven his car out of the gate the first passenger came along. She

was a pink toy cat with a very long tail and rather fierce whiskers. "Taxi-driver! I wish to be taken to the station please," she called to Noddy in a rather gruff voice.

"Certainly Madam, at your service!" said Noddy. He bowed gracefully and then bustled the pink cat into his little car. Noddy jumped into the driver's seat and laughed as he took the wheel. Oh, how happy he felt to be driving his own car!

"Hurry up, or I'll miss my train," said the toy cat, letting her long tail dangle over the side of the car. Noddy started up the engine. Mr Tubby, the next door neighbour, was watching out of his window. He saw the danger at once and shouted:

"Hey hey! Toy cat! Be careful now! Put your tail inside or it will get caught in the wheel!"

Noddy was so startled that he braked suddenly and the toy cat's hat fell off on to the road.

The cat picked up her hat, put her tail inside the car and looked rather crossly at Mr Tubby.

"I don't know what business it is of that teddy bear's!" she said.

Noddy drove off happily. Everyone shouted and waved as he sped down the road with the pink cat beside him.

"Look Noddy's got his first passenger!" they laughed. "He's a proper taxi-driver now!"

"Parp-parp!" said the hooter on Noddy's car proudly. A proper taxi-driver in a red and yellow taxi!

The car went over a bump and the cat's tail swung out again. Noddy saw it hanging over the side.

"Miss Cat, please put your tail back in the car," he said. "Really, I do wish cats would look after their tails better."

"It's my tail and I can do just what I like with it," hissed the cat, leaving it where it was. Noddy shrugged his shoulders and carefully drove through the woods to Toyland. At last he drove proudly into the station yard. He parked safely and politely helped the pink cat out of the car.

"My tail! I believe it's gone!" shouted the cat in dismay. Noddy stared at the toy cat. She did look very peculiar without a tail.

"Oh dear, I told you not to leave it hanging outside the car," he sighed as he searched for her tail.

There was a loud whistle as a brightly coloured toy train rushed into the station. Its carriages rumbled and clattered as it drew to a stop. The passengers jumped out and the wooden guard blew his whistle loudly.

"Quickly, or you'll miss your train," shouted Noddy. "Never

mind your tail, you can do without it
for a little while. Look…I haven't
got one and I manage very well."

"Don't be so silly!" wailed the cat
and she jumped into the carriage.

"I'll look for your tail!" shouted
Noddy as the train drew away
from the platform. His head nodded unhappily as he made his way
back to the car to start looking for

the pink tail. "What an awful start!" he sighed. Just then a large
teddy bear called to him from across the street:

"Taxi! Will you take me to Mr Tubby's house? I'm his brother."

Noddy was very pleased to have Mr Tubby's brother as a passenger, even though he was so large that he could only just squeeze into the car.

Noddy's car knew the way home and it simply whizzed down the cobbled streets of Toyland. All of a sudden Mr Teddy gave a loud yell.

"My hat's blown off! Stop, stop!"

Noddy put on the brake and the car came to a stop.

"You'll have to get out and find my hat," said Mr Tubby's brother. "I'm stuck fast in my seat."

Noddy searched everywhere but the hat was nowhere to be found. The big bear was very cross indeed. Noddy's head nodded sadly as he drove up to Mr Tubby's front door. Mrs Tubby came hurrying to the gate. "Hello, Teddy, hello," she cried. "Come on in!"

"I'll have to get out first!" growled Mr Teddy. "I'm stuck!"

They all pushed and pulled him, but in the end Noddy had to take the door off the car to let Mr Teddy out. He promised to replace the big bear's hat as soon as he could.

"You'd better," growled the bear and he walked away crossly, to say hello to Mrs Tubby.

"Oh dear," sighed Noddy as he fixed the door back on to his car. "I woke up so happy this morning and now I feel so sad."

Just as he finished, a doll carrying a big blue bag shouted to him from the bus stop across the road:

"Taxi! Will you take me to the railway station please?"

Noddy cheered up again. "Certainly Madam, right away!"

There was no room in the car for the doll's big blue bag so she balanced it on the back. Noddy drove very carefully.

"What a beautiful car!" said the doll. "Drive faster please, little nodding man...faster, faster!"

Noddy was pleased to show how fast his little car would go and he forgot all about the bag balanced on the back. When he got to the station...yes, you've guessed it, the bag had fallen off!

"What a careless taxi-driver!" said the doll crossly. "My train is about to leave, I haven't got time to go back now and look for it. Just promise me that you'll find my bag and put it on to the next train."

Tears came into Noddy's bright blue eyes as he watched the doll get into a carriage.

"I'm no good as a taxi-driver," he sobbed. "No good at all! Every time I get a passenger I lose something – first a tail, then a hat, now a bag. I think I'd better stop being a taxi-driver right away!"

Noddy sat in his car and wondered what to do next. Then he stopped crying and started to smile. He'd just had a good idea.

"I'll call on Big-Ears the brownie!" he thought. "He's lived in Toyland for a long time, he'll know what to do!"

Noddy drove to Big-Ears' toadstool house in the woods. When he arrived he tooted his horn loudly and Big-Ears came to answer the door.

"Noddy! How are you?" beamed Big-Ears. "I'm so glad you could call! I was just about to have tea – would you like some? How's your taxi business? Your car does look smart. I suppose you've had a lot of satisfied customers by now!"

"No I haven't," said Noddy gloomily. "I've had three unhappy passengers, and now *I'm* unhappy too."

Big-Ears was most astonished. "But why? What have you been doing to upset your passengers, Noddy?"

"Nothing except lose things," said Noddy and he told Big-Ears about the tail, the hat and the bag.

Big-Ears gave Noddy a hot cup of tea and some ginger cake and listened carefully to Noddy's story. He thought hard.

"Feel better now?" he smiled. "Good! Well, somebody must have found those things you lost. We'll go back to Toy Town and see if they've been handed in to Mr Plod at the police station."

"Of course! Let's go now!...or shall we wash up first?" asked Noddy excitedly.

"No. We'll go now," said Big-Ears. "I'm longing to have a ride in

your little car Noddy. I'll be your fourth passenger and bring you lots of good luck!"

They were soon speeding down the woodland path hooting the horn. Parp-parp!

"I don't want to frighten the rabbits!" shouted Noddy. "But we're in such a hurry today!"

When they arrived in Toyland, Noddy and Big-Ears called at the police station to see if the tail, the hat or the bag had been handed in to the lost property department.

"I'm sorry," sighed Mr Plod, "but nothing of that description has been handed in today. You never know, someone may have just picked these things up and be using them. Why don't you drive round the streets of Toy Town and see if you can find them?"

So that's just what they did. After a while they parked the car and went into the fairground. Suddenly Big-Ears tugged at Noddy's arm. He pointed at a clockwork mouse. Noddy stared. The mouse was wearing a pink scarf and was holding a big blue bag. He was talking loudly to a wooden rocking horse and was obviously very pleased with himself. Noddy listened.

"Yes, I'm going on holiday y'know. See this scarf and bag? I found them under a hedge. People go on holiday with bags like this don't they? So now I've got one, I'm going on holiday too." The mouse paused thoughtfully. "The only thing is, I don't know how to open the bag."

"Let me help!" said Big-Ears, walking up to the mouse. He un-wound the scarf from around the mouse's neck.

"Hmm," said Big-Ears. "This looks more like a cat's tail to me." Then he opened the bag, and read out the

name inside. "Angela Golden-Hair…as I thought!" said Big-Ears. "Now clockwork mouse, tell me what are you doing with Angela Golden-Hair's bag and the pink cat's tail?"

"I found them under a hedge!" snapped the mouse cheekily.

"But why didn't you go to the police station and give the things you found to…" began Big-Ears. But the mouse was gone, squeaking in fright and running as fast as his clockwork motor would carry him.

Noddy picked up the bag and wound the cat's tail round his neck to make sure he didn't lose it again!

The toy cat squealed when she opened the door of her cottage and saw Noddy standing there holding the pink tail she had lost.

"My tail!" she cried. "Oh Noddy, wait — I must give you a reward for your trouble. Thank you so much."

"No thank you!" smiled Noddy. "I should have looked after it for you better in the first place."

"I'm sure Noddy would appreciate the fare you owe him," interrupted Big-Ears stepping forward.

"Of course!" smiled the toy cat pressing two shiny pennies into Noddy's hand. "I shall always use your taxi when I want to go to the railway station."

Noddy was very pleased. He was so pleased that he sang all the way to the doll's house where Angela Golden-Hair lived. She opened the door and frowned, but then she jumped for joy.

"I never thought I'd get my best blue bag back!" she said. "Wait, you shall have a reward, Noddy."

"No thanks!" said Noddy. "It was my fault that it was lost."

"But I'm sure he'd accept the fare you owe him," winked Big-Ears.

"He shall have double!" laughed Angela, and she gave Noddy four shiny pennies. He could hardly believe his eyes. Four more pennies! "You're so honest and eager to please, I shall tell all my friends to use your taxi service from now on!" called the pretty doll.

"Well, well, Noddy. We are making progress," laughed Big-Ears. "Now to look for Mr Teddy's hat."

It was Noddy who saw the hat first! He was walking back past the funfair, gazing at the stalls and rides.

"The helter-skelter!" he shouted excitedly. "The hat's at the top of the helter-skelter!"

"Ha ha! Why, the wind must have blown it up there!" laughed Big-Ears. "Let's go and get it. Come on…race you to the top!"

Big-Ears won of course, because Noddy insisted on paying the entrance fee from the money he had earned as a taxi-driver.

"What a lovely view," sighed Noddy when he reached the top.

"Yes, you can see all over Toyland from here," smiled Big-Ears. "But there's no time to lose. We've got a delivery to make!"

With that, Big-Ears grabbed the hat and whizzed down the slide of the helter-skelter.

"This is fun!" laughed Noddy as he raced after him. "Oh won't Mr Teddy be pleased that we've found his hat! Now everything is back where it belongs!"

The bell on Noddy's hat almost played a tune as he drove through Toy Town. Noddy was driving very fast indeed.

"Be careful!" shouted Big-Ears, holding on to Mr Teddy's big hat. "I'll be losing my whiskers if you drive much faster!"

Noddy slowed down at once. It would be dreadful if Big-Ears lost something, too. Big-Ears grinned.

"It's all right," he laughed, "they grow very tightly. I shan't

really lose them at all!"

By the time they reached Mr Tubby's house Noddy felt very proud. He marched up to the bright yellow door and knocked loudly – blam, blam, blam!

Mr Teddy opened the door and grunted joyfully when he saw Noddy standing there holding his big hat.

"Please accept this with the compliments of Noddy's taxi service," smiled Noddy.

"Oh thank you Noddy!" growled the bear. "I've been hearing so many good things about you from my brother Mr Tubby. I want to apologise for being cross with you. Here's the fare I owe you. When I go home again, will you please take me back in your nice little car? I will pay you well."

"Oh yes sir, right away," beamed Noddy.

When he arrived back at his House-for-One Noddy was even happier than he had been that morning.

"Look, Big-Ears, six more pennies. Aren't I lucky?"

"Well, you deserve them Noddy," smiled Big-Ears. "Your taxi service is a good one. Tomorrow we'll buy a big box of bricks with the money you've earned and I'll help you to build a

fine garage for your car."

A proper garage! Noddy was too happy for words.

"Come on then!" he giggled. "Jump into my car and we'll go and buy some supper. It's a lovely evening, Big-Ears. It won't rain. I'm sure my little car won't get wet tonight."

They laughed and sang all the way to the shops. Big-Ears was happy because he had put things right for his friend, and Noddy was happy because all his customers were satisfied at last.

The next morning Noddy met Big-Ears at the toy brick warehouse. They bought the best box of brightly coloured bricks they could find and a strong belt to strap them safely onto the back of the car. Noddy drove home very carefully. Mr Tubby was waiting and helped them to unload the box.

In no time they had built the prettiest garage in Toyland.

"Parp-parp," hooted the car as Noddy drove it into its new home. Noddy stood back to admire his work.

"What a lovely garage" he laughed. "And I've still got three shiny pennies left over from the money I've earned."

"That's good," laughed Big-Ears. "We deserve a treat!" With that, he carefully peeled the gold paper from one of the coins.

"All the pennies in Toyland are chocolate ones," he laughed.
"Try one for yourself, Noddy."

"Oh, I do like Toyland," said Noddy as he bit into the chocolate. "Do you suppose I'll have lots more adventures here?"

"Yes," said Big-Ears, "I'm sure you will!"